Ronald Morgan Goes to Bat

Ronald Morgan Goes to Bat

by Patricia Reilly Giff • illustrated by Susanna Natti

Puffin Books

Special thanks to Hobie Summers

PUFFIN BOOKS
Published by the Penguin Group
Penguin Putnam Books for Young Readers,
345 Hudson Street, New York, New York 10014, U.S.A.
Penguin Books Ltd, 27 Wrights Lane, London W8 5TZ, England
Penguin Books Australia Ltd, Ringwood, Victoria, Australia
Penguin Books Canada Ltd, 10 Alcorn Avenue, Toronto, Ontario, Canada M4V 3B2
Penguin Books (N.Z.) Ltd, 182-190 Wairau Road, Auckland 10, New Zealand
Penguin Books Ltd, Registered Offices: Harmondsworth, Middlesex, England

First published in the United States of America by Viking Penguin,
a division of Penguin Books USA Inc., 1988
Published in Picture Puffins, 1990
29   30   28
Text copyright © Patricia Reilly Giff, 1988
Illustrations copyright © Susanna Natti, 1988
All rights reserved

LIBRARY OF CONGRESS CATALOGING IN PUBLICATION DATA
Giff, Patricia Reilly.
Ronald Morgan goes to bat / Patricia Reilly Giff ;
pictures by Susanna Natti.   p.   cm.
Summary: Although he can't hit or catch, Ronald Morgan loves to play baseball.
ISBN 978-0-14-050669-3
[1. Baseball—Fiction.]   I. Natti, Susanna, ill.   II. Title.
[PZ7.G3626Ro   1990]   [E]—dc20   89-37885

Manufactured in China   Set in Aster.

With love to my son Jim, the father
P.R.G.

To Napa and Elke and Lakka
and to the people who loved them.

S.N.

Baseball started today.

Mr. Spano said everyone could play.

"Even me?" I asked.

And Tom said,

"You're letting Ronald Morgan play?

He can't hit, he can't catch.

He can't do anything."

Mr. Spano looked at me.

"Everyone," he said.

"Yahoo!" I yelled.

I pulled on my red and white shirt,
the one that says GO TEAM GO,
and ran outside to the field.
"Two things," Mr. Spano told us.
"Try hard, and keep your eye on the ball."

Then it was time to practice.

Michael was up first.

He smacked the ball with the bat.

The ball flew across the field.

"Good," said Mr. Spano.

"Great, Slugger!" I yelled.

"We'll win every game."

It was my turn next.
I put on the helmet,
and stood at home plate.
"Ronald Morgan," said Rosemary.
"You're holding the wrong end
of the bat."
Quickly I turned it around.
I clutched it close to the end.

10

Whoosh went the first ball.
Whoosh went the second one.
Wham went the third.

It hit me in the knee.
"Are you all right?" asked Michael.
But I heard Tom say,
"I knew it.
Ronald Morgan's the worst."

At snack time,
we told Miss Tyler about the team.
"I don't hit very well," I said.
And Rosemary said,
"The ball hits him instead."
Everybody laughed, even me.
I shook my head.
"I hope it doesn't happen again."
Miss Tyler gave me some raisins.
"You have to hit the ball
before it hits you," she said.

We played every day.

I tried hard, but the ball came fast.

I closed my eyes and swung.

"If only he could hit the ball once,"
Rosemary said.

And Billy shook his head.

I couldn't tell them I was afraid of
the ball.

"Go team go," I whispered.

One day, the team sat on the grass.
We watched the third grade play.
They were big, they were strong,
they were good.
Johnny hit a home run,
and Joy tagged a man out.

"We'll never hit like that," said Tom.

And Rosemary said,

"We'll never catch like that either."

But I said,

"Our team is the best."

Mr. Spano nodded.

"That's the spirit, Ronald."

Mr. Spano told us,
"Now we'll run the bases."
Rosemary, you can go first."
Rosemary went fast.
She raced for first base.
"Terrific, Speedy!" I yelled.

"Let me go next," I said.

"I can do that, too."

But the field was muddy.

My sneaker came off.

Jimmy said, "That kid's running
bases the wrong way."

And Tom yelled, "Ronald Morgan.
You're heading for third base."

The next day, we worked on catching.
I was out in left field.
While I waited, I found a stick,
and started to scratch out the mud.
I wrote G for go.
I wrote G for great.
Our team is the best, I thought.
Then I wrote H for hit.
H for home run.
If only I could do that.

Just then I heard yelling.

Someone had hit the ball.

"Catch it, Ronald!" Tom shouted.

I put down the stick.

I put up my mitt.

Too late.

The ball sailed into the trees.

Mr. Spano took us for ice cream.

"You deserve it for trying," he said.

"Our team is really good."

I had a chocolate cone.

Michael's a slugger, I thought.

And Rosemary can really run.

But I'm still afraid of the ball.

On the way home,

we saw some kids playing ball.

"Want to hit a few?" Michael asked.

I shook my head.

"Maybe I won't play ball anymore."

Michael said, "We need you.

You have spirit.

You help the team feel good."

"But how can we win?" I asked.

"I can't even hit the ball."

I saw my father and ran to catch up.

"See you, Michael," I said.

My father asked, "How's the champ?"

"I'm the worst," I said.

"I was the worst, too," said my father.

"But then..."

"What?"

My father laughed. "I stopped closing
my eyes when I swung."

"Maybe that's what I do."

"How about a little practice?" he asked.

We went into the yard.

My father threw me some balls.

I missed the first one...

I missed the second.

And then...

I opened my eyes and swung.
Crack went the ball.
"Ouch!" went my father.
"You hit me in the knee."
"Home run!" yelled my mother.

"Sorry," I said.

"Hey, I did it!"

My father rubbed his knee.

"You certainly did," he said.

I ran to pick up the ball.
"See you later," I said.
My father smiled.
"Where are you going?"
I grabbed the bat.
"Some kids are playing ball.
I think I'll hit a few."

I looked back.
"And you know what else?
I guess I'll stay on the team.
I have spirit...
and sometimes I can hit the ball.
Mike was right.
I think they need me."